EMMETT AND JEZ

Also by Hannah Shaw

KITTEN LADY'S BIG BOOK OF LITTLE KITTENS

Adventures in Fosterland series
SUPER SPINACH

• KITTEN LADY •
HANNAH SHAW

Adventures in FOSTERLAND

Illustrated by
BEV JOHNSON

EMMETT AND JEZ

Aladdin
New York   London   Toronto   Sydney   New Delhi

ALADDIN
An imprint of Simon & Schuster Children's Publishing Division
1230 Avenue of the Americas, New York, New York 10020
First Aladdin paperback edition June 2022
Copyright © 2022 by Kitten Lady, LLC
Also available in an Aladdin hardcover edition.
All rights reserved, including the right of reproduction in whole or in part in any form.
ALADDIN and related logo are registered trademarks of Simon & Schuster, Inc.
For information about special discounts for bulk purchases, please contact
Simon & Schuster Special Sales at 1-866-506-1949 or business@simonandschuster.com.
The Simon & Schuster Speakers Bureau can bring authors to your live event. For more
information or to book an event contact the Simon & Schuster Speakers Bureau
at 1-866-248-3049 or visit our website at www.simonspeakers.com.
Designed by Tiara Iandiorio
The illustrations for this book were rendered digitally.
The text of this book was set in Banda.
Manufactured in the United States of America 0422 OFF
2 4 6 8 10 9 7 5 3 1
Library of Congress Cataloging-in-Publication Data
Names: Shaw, Hannah René, 1987- author. | Johnson, Beverly, illustrator.
Title: Emmett and Jez / by Hannah Shaw ; illustrated by Bev Johnson.
Description: First Aladdin paperback edition. | New York : Aladdin, 2022. |
Series: Adventures in Fosterland | Summary: When the piglet Emmett arrives in
Fosterland, he relies on a three-legged kitten named Jez to show him the ropes.
Identifiers: LCCN 2021023108 (print) | LCCN 2021023109 (ebook) |
ISBN 9781665901192 (hc) | ISBN 9781665901185 (pbk) | ISBN 9781665901208 (ebook)
Subjects: CYAC: Pigs—Fiction. | Cats—Fiction. | Animals—Infancy—Fiction. |
Foster care of animals—Fiction. | Friendship—Fiction.
Classification: LCC PZ7.1.S4935 Em 2022 (print) |
LCC PZ7.1.S4935 (ebook) | DDC [Fic]—dc23
LC record available at https://lccn.loc.gov/2021023108
LC ebook record available at https://lccn.loc.gov/2021023109

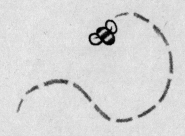

For every pig who dreams of a
happy future

Contents

CHAPTER 1

Bee Careful

Thud!

The whole world seemed to be spinning around Emmett as he hit the pavement and rolled into a ditch. *Ouch. That hurt!*

Little Emmett brushed himself off and lifted his head, which was now throbbing, and squinted as he watched a truck disappear into the distance. It all happened so fast. One minute he was squeezed into a truck packed with his mama and siblings, and the next he was tumbling down the interstate, all alone.

Alone. What a terrible feeling! All his (short) life, he'd known the comfort of friends nuzzling against him and the familiar sounds of the barnyard. Now he sat trembling, nothing to keep him company but the whoosh of cars speeding past.

And so there he sat, on the side of the road, waiting for someone to find him. He wasn't sure who he was waiting for or where he wanted to go—he just knew that he didn't belong *here*. His hooves were scuffed, his tummy was making rumbly sounds, and his mouth felt drier than sand. He was only a baby, no taller than the dandelions that surrounded him. For a long while, he sat there under those yellow petals, waiting and squealing.

And waiting. And squealing.

Then, just feet away, a bumblebee landed on a flower petal. Emmett leapt up to call out to her.

"Help! Please, help! I was in one of those . . . zoomy things . . . and I've fallen . . . and . . . I've lost my way! I've been sitting here alone all afternoon. Can you point me in the right direction?"

Stunned, the bumblebee quickly stuffed her pockets with pollen and flew toward him, landing right on the tip of his fuzzy pink snout.

"Why, it'zzz a baby pig!" the bumblebee said.

"A baby *what*?" Emmett paused, wondering whether he'd ever heard the word "pig" before.

"Hmm," he said as he looked cross-eyed at the bee with big dark eyes peeking out from under long curly eyelashes. "I'm afraid I don't know anything about a baby pig," he said. "I'm just Emmett. But can you help me?"

"Oh dear," the bumblebee replied. "Thizzz izzz no place for a baby pig."

Emmett wiggled his snout in confusion. The truth is that he did not know

who he was or *where* he belonged. All
he knew was that he was himself, a little
guy as tall as a flower, with a rumbly
belly and nowhere to go.

The bee looked west toward the sun
and gasped. "Oh dear! I'm afraid I have
important bizzzness to attend to," she

said, realizing that she was soon due back at the hive. "Little pig, bee careful!" the bumblebee shouted, and flew off with a gust of wind.

"Wait! Come back! Don't leave me here!" Emmett called, but it was too late. The bee was out of sight. *Sheesh, she sure was flighty,* Emmett thought, and flopped against the grass, wondering if he'd be alone forever.

Oh, how he hated to be alone.

The sun was scorching, and he was *thirsty.* Getting up, Emmett tiptoed along a thin yellow line, trying to make his way toward a puddle shining in the distance. Cars zipped past, honking and blowing hot wind against his side. Emmett was scared, and if *this* was what it meant to be a pig, he longed to be anyone else—and anywhere else. Finally, he made it to the puddle, and as he drank, he saw in his reflection a fuzzy pink baby looking back at him. He shuddered. "I don't think I like being a baby pig at all."

Screeeech! A car came to a sudden stop, and he jolted, splashing water all over himself, as the door opened wide. Emmett backed away slowly as a long shadow fell over him, blocking the sunshine. As if out of thin air, two huge hands wrapped around his tiny body, lifting him toward the sky.

He couldn't believe his eyes. He was being held by a giant!

Before he knew what was happening,
Emmett was sitting in a box on the passenger seat, the trees zooming past his
face as if he were flying through space at
the speed of light. His mind was racing.
Who was this giant? Where was she taking him? And most importantly . . . would
there be snacks?

CHAPTER 2

Uncharted Territory

The trees finally stopped moving and the giant plopped a dizzy Emmett before a door that must have been one thousand feet tall. *Gulp.* He could feel butterflies in his stomach as he wondered what might be on the other side. The door creaked open, and Emmett placed one hoof inside to take a first peek at the mysterious new space. *Here goes nothing*, he thought.

Tip-tap, tip-tap . . . slip! His tiny hooves slid awkwardly across the tile. He caught his breath and shook his head, getting his feet back under him. *What a curious terrain!*

Tippy-tappy, tippy-tappy, he carefully continued ahead.

Emmett felt uncertain about this strange place but was relieved to be off the side of the road. *Anything is better than that awful ditch*, he thought. *Besides, maybe I can find someone here to ask for help finding something to eat. . . .*

He squinted. At the end of the hallway, he saw a small fuzzy mouse.

"Hello?" he called out to the mouse, but the mouse did not respond.

"Could you tell me where I am? I was by a busy road, and I talked to a bee who flew right off! Next thing I knew, I got scooped up by this giant . . . and now . . . well, I think that I might be even more lost than before. I just need someone to tell me where to go, or at least where I can find some food," he continued.

The mouse stayed silent and perfectly still. Why was it so hard to find someone to talk to?

Emmett approached the mouse, who had beady little eyes but didn't blink at all. He nudged it with his snout, and it flipped onto its side, making a funny rattling sound. *Huh.* He nudged it harder, and it tumbled down the hall. Emmett jumped back. "You're not even real! You're . . . made of fabric!"

He pattered farther down the hallway. A poof of colorful feathers lay across the path, and he ran toward them. "Excuse me, Mr. Bird, can you tell me—" But just then he noticed the feathers were glued to a bouncy ball, and there was no bird to be found. He furrowed his brow. *What is going on here?*

Sitting still, he could hear nothing but the rumbling of his stomach, which was getting louder by the minute. But as he listened closely, there was a distant clanging noise in another room. He peeked around the corner and saw that the giant had placed a bowl on the ground . . . and she was pouring some kind of yummy-looking creamy liquid into the dish!

Emmett's nose wiggled wildly. *Could it be?* He stepped closer, sniffing the sweet-smelling air. The scent was irresistible. He ran up to the dish, took a deep whiff, and squealed.

FOOD!

Wasting no time, Emmett jumped into the air and did a belly flop straight into the pond of warm milk. He splashed through the sloshy puddle, slurping it up. Curling his tongue like a straw, he ate as fast as he could. As he was guzzling down his first meal all day, he managed to get food on his feet . . . and all over his belly . . . and even on the top of his head.

Within what seemed like no time at all, the dish was nearly empty. As he licked little drizzles from his chin, a new feeling came over Emmett, and he paused, pondering what was happening in his belly, which was feeling funny and tight. *This* was the feeling of having had enough to eat, but he hadn't felt anything like that ever before, so even though he was *very full*, he couldn't help trying to fit another droplet into his mouth. When he couldn't drink another lick, he plopped onto his side with a *thump*, stretching his chunky belly across the saucer.

Maybe this place isn't so bad after all, he thought.

With a big stretch, he turned his sight to the land before him and surveyed the area in search of a comfy spot to nap.

First he tried to lie on a pile of blankets. But the blankets were lumpy, and even when he nudged them with his snout to try to make a cozy bed, he just couldn't get comfortable.

Next he flopped atop what he *thought* was a flower bed. It might have been the perfect size for his little body, but when he took a deep inhale, the funky smell of feet was too much.

After that he tried sprawling out on the floor, but the cool tile gave him a chill.

Brr! All he wanted was a warm place to curl up and sleep!

Emmett looked to the window, and

there it was: the most comfortable place on planet Earth.

A pink cloud floating in the warmth of a shining sunbeam. Rays of light were glittering like pixie dust in the air, showering down on the fluffy pillow, which looked squishy and smooshy and absolutely scrumptious.

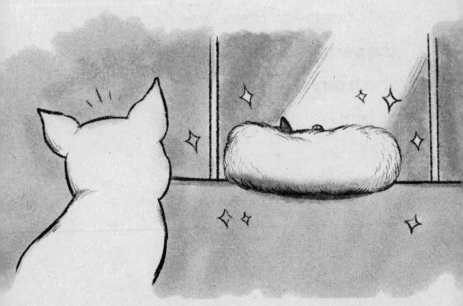

Time stood still as Emmett trotted toward the magical pink cloud, his eyes wide with wonder. He ran and ran, ready to make a dive for it and leap belly first into the cloudy cushion. But just as his little hooves began their liftoff, he saw something that stopped him in his tracks. *Skrrrrrt!*

He gulped. There was a creature on the pillow . . . a creature with shiny, razor-sharp claws. And they were pointed right at him!

CHAPTER 3

A Magical Place

Sniff, sniff, sniff.

At the edge of the cloud appeared a little brown nose, wiggling with long white whiskers.

Sniff, sniff, sniff.

Emmett braced himself as the fluffy cloud-dweller leaned forward, sniffing in his direction until they were snout-to-snoot.

Up from the cloud rose a fuzzy indi-
vidual with brown fur and big blue eyes.
"So you're the new kid, huh?" he said.
"Yeah, I was the new kid last week . . .
which was practically *ages ago*. So I
guess this makes me the big guy! Okay,
kid, hop in." He scooted to the side to
make room for Emmett.

Stunned, Emmett sat perfectly still, staring up at the being, who tapped his back paw and said, "Well? Are you going to come hang out or not?"

Emmett shyly stepped into the bed, relieved to finally find someone who wanted to talk to him. "I'm Emmett. I've had such a confusing day." His voice grew stronger as he spoke. "I was on the side of the road, and it was so scary there, and now all of a sudden I'm here . . . but I'm afraid I don't know where *here* is!"

The fluffy being raised an eyebrow. "You mean to tell me that you don't know where you are right now?" He sat up tall—showing off his long, shiny tiger-striped coat—and cleared his throat before breaking into a speech.

"Ahem!" he began. "Hear ye, hear ye! I am Jez, and this kingdom you have entered . . . is Fosterland," he said, gesturing grandly with his furry arms outstretched.

"Fosterland," Jez continued, "is where the lost are found, the sick are healed, and the hungry are fed and loved. My friend, you have just entered a magical place where you can lie back and relax, enjoy the buffet, and focus on your own personal growth. Fosterland is a haven for foster kittens like you and me."

Retreat? Food? Love? Emmett liked

what he was hearing. His ears perked up. "I'm a . . . foster kitten?"

"Yes, genius." Jez laughed and rolled his eyes. "Gosh, you *are* new, huh? *Of course* you're a foster kitten. We both are! Consider yourself lucky, because us foster kittens have it good in Fosterland."

Emmett leaned in, listening. He could feel the corners of his mouth curling into a tiny smile. Maybe this was his lucky day, and he wasn't a little pig after all! This Jez character seemed like he probably knew what he was talking about—he was bigger, older, and carried himself like a proud lion. Emmett sat like a perfect student, taking little notes in his mind. *Note to self: I'm a foster kitten, and I have it good now.*

Stretching his neck to appear as tall as possible, Jez continued. "There was a time when I was in your shoes, little one, so wide-eyed and new to the world. And a sleek black cat, much older and wiser, spoke to me in rhyme:

"'Dream big, dream big, and soon you'll see, all that a foster grows to be . . .'"

He held his paw to his heart, closing his eyes as if in deep reflection (but really, he was just trying to remember the rest of the words).

". . . 'The dream inside your heart'. . . something . . .

"Hmm . . .

"Something about dreams and hearts . . ."

The truth was, he was so excited to have a new friend that he could not remember the rest of the rhyme.

He paused, took a deep breath, then lowered his head until he was eye-to-eye with Emmett, whispering in quiet amazement: "Legend has it that all the dreams you have as a baby in Fosterland come true once you are big and grown."

Emmett teared up a little as Jez continued his monologue, marching back and forth like a fluffy soldier with a swishy tail.

"Little kitten, you are tiny. But someday you will be mighty. And *that* is why you are here in Fosterland. That is why we are *both* here. To grow into mighty cats! As you can see, I'm well on my way. . . ."

Watching as Jez strutted in a circle, Emmett was speechless. Jez was shining with sophistication! Then Emmett looked down at his little pink feet, which were still scuffed with dirt from the side of the road. He thought about how scary it had felt to be lost and how good it felt to be in Fosterland. And he decided that it was a very good thing to be a foster kitten indeed.

Even if he was a little smaller than Jez, Emmett was bubbling with the happy feeling that maybe they really were quite the same—each with two eyes, two

ears, and one loving, tender heart. The
only difference, as far as he could tell,
was that Jez only had three legs, while
Emmett had four.

"What happened to your leg?"
Emmett asked.

"I used to have four legs," Jez replied,
"but one of them got hurt when I was

a baby. That's how I ended up here in Fosterland—I needed a place to heal. But don't worry, I get around just fine on three legs. See?" And with that he leapt over Emmett's head, landing on a short bench overlooking the cloud. Now Emmett really did feel small.

Jez looked down at Emmett, who was sinking into the squishiness of the pink cloud. He said, "You look a little different, too. What happened to your tail?"

My tail? Emmett thought to himself, rolling around the bed to try to get a view of his behind. Emmett's tail was short, skinny, pink, and nearly hairless. When he was excited, it wagged back and forth uncontrollably, like a flag in the wind. It was nothing like Jez's tail, which was long, fluffy, and swishing through the air with grace.

Emmett had no memory of his tail ever looking like Jez's. But, wanting to fit in, he replied, "Oh, my tail? Uh . . . yeah, same thing. Something happened. Yeah."

"I get it," Jez said, hopping back down and placing a loving paw on Emmett's back. "It's okay to look a little different— that's what makes you special."

Emmett exhaled a sigh of relief after what had been a long, confusing day. Settling in by Jez's side, he kicked his little hooves to the side and felt his worries melting away. He'd never sat next to a kitten before, but it sure was comfy. Jez was as soft as a fleece pillow and seemed to be vibrating gently like the motor of a truck. He remembered his previous snuggle buddies and hoped that wherever they'd ended up, they'd found a Fosterland for themselves, too.

"What's that fluttering sound in your chest?" Emmett asked.

"I'm purring. That's what us kittens do when we're happy," Jez replied, curling into a cozy crescent. "I'm glad you're here, Emmett. I've been waiting for a foster friend like you."

Emmett cuddled in close, listening to the purrs. *So this is what happiness sounds like*, he thought, wondering if he might someday learn how to purr, too. He closed his eyes, and the rumbling sounds soothed him right to sleep.

CHAPTER 4

The Grand Tour

In the morning, Jez and Emmett awoke tangled together in a puddle of cuddles. Jez stretched his arms around Emmett and asked, "Do you like cat jokes?"

"I don't know any. Tell me one!" he replied.

"Okay. Here's one: What do you call a pile of kittens?" Jez said, flopping his furry body over Emmett.

Emmett paused. He had no idea.

". . . A meowntain! Bahaha!" Jez cracked himself up, and Emmett chuckled too, even though he wasn't totally sure he got the joke.

"Here's another one. What does a cat read in the morning?"

Emmett was quiet again.

". . . The mewspaper! Get it? *Mews?*" Emmett didn't really get it, but it didn't matter—both of them were laughing hysterically. It was just fun to have someone to laugh with!

"I do have one question," Emmett asked, thinking about everything that happened the day before. "Have you ever seen a giant around here?"

"A giant. Hmm. Let me think. . . . Oh, do you mean the food fairy?" Jez replied. "Yeah, she's cool. I know she's as big as a monster, but she's very gentle. And kind. She's the one who gives us all the snacks, and let me tell you, she gives chin scratches that'll knock you right out! Yep, she's a cool lady all right. . . . Except there is one weird thing about her." Jez paused, looking from side to side as if he were about to let Emmett in on a secret. "Sometimes . . . she steals my poop."

Emmett giggled. "She does *what*?! Weird. So weird." A gigantic fairy who steals your poop and leaves food behind? That was so silly! But at least there was nothing to fear.

Emmett's tummy rumbled and Jez's rumbled right back, so they headed over to the kitchen, where the food fairy was making breakfast. Perfect timing! Fresh food flowed like a wondrous waterfall onto a dish, and Emmett began sloshing and spinning and lapping it up with glee. Jez was more proper with his dining style and preferred instead to drink his formula from a bottle. Ears wiggling as he drank, Jez kept one eye on his fuzzy pink pal, who was tap dancing with all four legs on the plate.

"That must be good stuff," Jez laughed. "Mind if I try some?" Jez took a lick of what Emmett was eating, and even though it looked like his meal, it tasted very strange. "Yuck," he blurted out, and went back to gulping from the bottle until it was empty.

Grooming his paws and licking his lips, Jez was almost clean when Emmett started shaking his full belly from side to side, sending droplets flying all around. "Oops, sorry!" He giggled.

Jez's face was dotted with slop . . . but it was all too funny to be mad about! They both laughed it off and continued to groom themselves in their own ways.

"Come with me. I'll give you the grand tour of Fosterland," Jez said proudly after they were both clean. "I know this place like the back of my paw!"

Emmett trotted along behind his tour guide, looking around and oinking under his breath. He was so excited to begin the day with his new pal. Fosterland seemed to be a safe place for him—with no danger of cars, or unhelpful bees, or loneliness—and Emmett couldn't wait to see more.

They zipped through the kingdom, and soon the ground beneath their feet shifted to a new and interesting texture, with little strands of fiber popping up all around. "We've reached the first destination on our tour. The grasslands. The floor here feels nice and squishy between your toe beans."

Emmett didn't have toe beans, but he *did* have an itchy butt, and it turned out that a carpet was the perfect place to scratch it. Emmett shimmied back and forth, shaking his booty all along the floor. "Wow, this is awesome!" he said. "Try it!"

Jez giggled and gave it a shot. The two of them wiggled across the rug, looking like a couple of squirmy worms dancing to their favorite music. "Woo-hoo! Scratching your butt is awesome!" Jez said, and they high-fived.

Emmett spotted a crinkly ball across the way and ran toward it at full speed, bopping it across the floor with his snout. "Think fast!" he called out as he hurled the ball toward Jez, who leapt into the air and pounced atop the toy.

The two of them dribbled the ball back and forth—Emmett with his nose and Jez with his paws—chasing and pouncing and laughing with glee. "Soccer is a foster kitten favorite!" Jez exclaimed.

As they moved along, they entered a tropical zone. "Ooh, this is another land-mark for you to know about. This is the sun box," Jez explained. "Us babies need to stay warm. If you ever feel chilly, you just come over here and sun your buns!"

Emmett smiled and closed his eyes as he stood in front of the heater, which was sending warmth into the room. "I could get used to this," he said, melting into a happy little puddle.

Prancing along, Jez continued with his tour. "Oh, and over here is Mount Couch. It's not easy to get to the top, but I hear once you reach it, the view is awesome."

Emmett looked from side to side but

didn't see Mount Couch. "Where is it? I don't see any mountain."

"Look up!" Jez said.

"What's 'up'?" Emmett replied.

"Not too much. How about you?" Jez laughed and laughed. "No, really, do you mean to tell me you've never looked up?" he asked, gesturing toward the sky with his paws.

Emmett strained his neck to the side. The truth is, he was about as bendy as a raw potato, so it was hard for him to look toward the ceiling. He spent almost all his time focusing on the ground level, so it had never even occurred to him that there were things higher than his line of sight. Twisting his chunky body, he got a quick glimpse of the mountaintop, and he oinked with surprise. "Wow! There's an up!"

"Oh yeah, big-time. And us cats are all about 'up.' I for one can't wait to be big enough to climb Mount Couch."

Us cats are all about "up," Emmett thought to himself. *Noted.*

They continued exploring different rooms as Jez showed Emmett all the coolest spots in Fosterland. Over the slippery tiles, through the long hallways, into the cracks and crevices where all the cat toys go to hide. They snuck into the sneakiest of spots, and Jez warned of the dangers in the land.

"Don't chew the snakes that come

out of the wall. That's one thing the food fairy *really* does not like. I know how tempting it is, because we are hunters, but listen . . . just don't chew the snakes, okay?" Emmett looked at the snakes, and he had no desire to chew them anyway.

"Next stop: the rain forest!" Jez said, raising his eyebrows and gesturing grandly. "Right this way. Here we have a region with rather humid weather and a frequent pattern of precipitation. Once a day it rains hot water from the corner over there, and—get this—the food fairy stands right underneath the stream! It's a little strange, but it always smells like fresh flowers afterward, so it's kind of nice if you ask me. Seems like the rain must have just stopped . . . ," he said, checking the air with a raised paw.

As Emmett entered the bathroom, he stumbled upon a big mirror, which was foggy with steam. He glanced into the glass and saw a blobby pink shape. He scooted away from it. He didn't want to remember being a pig, or how it felt to be sitting on the side of that busy road. His pig days were *over*. He was a foster kitten now!

"What's next?" Emmett asked as he sprinted quickly out of the room.

"I suppose I should tell you about the wise black panther you'll see sometimes," Jez said, gesturing toward a shiny black cat resting against a windowpane.

"That's Coco the Elder Cat. Her amber eyes have witnessed the whole history of this land, and she knows truths you and I can't even begin to understand. She's kind of . . . a historian of sorts. But you mustn't bother her. She only speaks to us foster kittens when the time is right."

Coco the Elder Cat peered in their direction, and Emmett nodded shyly. "Understood."

They walked around the corner and saw the food fairy opening a large brown package. "Oh, buddy. I've got a huge surprise for you," Jez said, his eyes wide. "Have you ever seen a cardboard box?"

"No. What *is* it? What's inside?"

Emmett asked. Jez seemed to know so much, and Emmett knew so little, but he couldn't wait to know more.

"Oh, the food fairy receives these big brown boxes full of stuff that she thinks we need, but honestly, it's not about what's inside the box. It's about *the box*. Just wait until you see how cool these things are!"

They bounced over to the box, which the food fairy had opened. Inside, it was filled with carpeted squares and scratching posts, which meant absolutely nothing to Emmett and Jez. "You have to ask yourself why they would ruin a perfectly good box by filling it with all this nonsense," Jez said.

The food fairy pulled out the different parts and began screwing them together, building something. But Emmett and Jez cared only about one thing.

Diving into the empty cardboard!

"It's a wrestling ring! Come on in, if you dare!" Jez teased, hopping swiftly inside the box.

Emmett tried to enter with one smooth jump, but his tummy got caught on the side, so he tumble-fell into the box, head over hooves. Inside this exciting new arena, he could feel his inner fighter starting to emerge.

He huffed and puffed. Jez wiggled his butt.

"Oh, it's on!"

Emmett ran full speed at Jez, but Jez hopped out of the way. Emmett spun around and around, bumping his blocky head into Jez. Jez pounced on Emmett's back with both front paws, and Emmett squealed and stomped in a circle, full of energy. "Catch me if you can!"

Jez and Emmett were darting around the box, wrestling, nibbling, and chasing. They were a surprisingly even pair. Sure, Jez had claws, but Emmett had a strong snout that packed a powerful punch. It was anyone's match!

Jez came in with a left-paw swipe, then bunny-kicked Emmett in the belly with his back foot. Emmett's little legs were wiggling and wiggling until he

broke free and then headbutted Jez
straight into the air until he thought he
would hit the ceiling! Jez landed on all
three legs and held out one paw.

"Tie?" Jez panted.

"Tie," agreed Emmett, who was both
beaming and totally out of breath.

They flopped against the cardboard

and lay in the box side by side, exhila-
rated and exhausted. Jez draped his arm
over Emmett and said, "You know what,
Emmett? You're my best friend."

"You're my best friend, too," Emmett
oinked with a smile.

The food fairy reached into the box
with one giant hand and gave chin

scratches to Jez, who was leaning into her hand. With the other hand, she began to rub Emmett's tummy, and he promptly rolled sideways and closed his eyes. In his mind was just one thought: *I wish that I could feel this happy forever.*

Jez looked over to his friend, who seemed to enjoy being scratched in weird places like his belly, chest, and even his armpits! "Doesn't that tickle?" Jez whispered, but Emmett was zoned out, and with his eyes closed, he answered only with a smile. Swept up in the comforting feeling of friendship and belly rubs, he let out a peaceful sigh and drifted off to sleep.

CHAPTER 5

New Heights

Yawn! Emmett stretched out his hooves over the edge of the fluffy cloud bed as beams of light shone down on another day in Fosterland. He'd watched the sun rise and fall several times now, and he was starting to feel right at home. But each morning, he couldn't help but notice that the bed was somehow getting smaller. He rolled to his side, squishing Jez slightly. "Sorry! Sheesh, does it seem like the bed is shrinking?" Emmett muttered.

Jez peeled himself out from underneath Emmett's belly, which had squashed his hair flat against his body and revealed that underneath all that long fur, he was actually a little smaller than his friend now. "You're just growing," Jez said as he shook his body, fluffing out his coat. "We both are!"

Emmett wasn't so sure how to feel about growing, but if Jez was okay with it, then he supposed it must be all right. As long as he was still a foster kitten in Fosterland with Jez, Emmett felt like everything would be just fine.

After gobbling up breakfast side by side, Jez told Emmett, "Today's the big day. The day we try to climb Mount Couch. Are you with me?"

Emmett felt a squiggly feeling in his tummy. Was it nerves, or had he over-eaten? Either way, he was feeling uncertain about this whole *climbing* ordeal, but he didn't want to let his friend down. Emmett nodded, and Jez began to prepare him for the journey.

"Emmett, this is a feat only a truly skilled kitten can achieve. If we're going to do this right, we have to start by training. Follow me." As if he were teaching a gym class, Jez began to lunge and stretch, calling out orders to Emmett, who was trying desperately to keep up. "Aaaand lunge and stretch, and lunge and stretch. Let's really see those claws, Emmett! Pick up the pace!"

Emmett felt silly, but he lunged none-theless, looking down at his toes, which were hooved—not clawed. "I'm not so sure about this," Emmett said as he tripped over himself.

But Jez kept on going. "Okay, next we need to practice our leaps. If we're going to scale Mount Couch, we're going to need to be able to hop pretty high. Let's hop together on the count of three. One . . . two . . . three . . . hop!"

Jez rocketed into the air, while Emmett barely got all four feet off the ground. "I tried my best," Emmett said, shrugging.

"Well, I feel ready. . . . Let's give it a shot," Jez said, and the two of them headed to the foothills of the mountain.

Jez enthusiastically leapt as high as he could, but when his feet touched the mountain, he just slid down the side. After trying a few more times, he tried something else. Giving himself a running start, he jumped straight into the air and released his sharp claws, digging them into the side of the cliff. Hanging there, he pulled with all his might to try to lift his body toward the mountaintop. He tried . . . and tried . . . but he was too small. He just couldn't make it to the top.

"Okay, Emmett, you next," Jez said, trying to catch his breath.

"I don't know. . . . You seem a little more cut out for this climbing stuff than I do," Emmett muttered. But Jez begged him to give it a shot, so he sighed. "Okay, here goes nothing."

Emmett moved back and ran full speed ahead, thrusting his body upward with all his might . . . but he barely jumped an inch off the floor before crashing snout-first into the side of the mountain.

Ouch!

"I have an idea," Jez said with a glimmer in his eye. "Emmett, you're really sturdy. I'll climb on your back, and then

I'll be so much closer to the top of Mount Couch!"

Jez hopped on Emmett's back, and with a dream and a whoosh, he jumped right to the tippy-top of Mount Couch. "We did it! Well . . . I did it!" Jez exclaimed.

"What's it look like from up there?" Emmett asked.

"Dude, it's incredible. You can see everything! The sun box, the grasslands, the wrestling ring . . . even the rain forest! I'm the king of the world!" Jez felt so accomplished as he peered across Fosterland. Being high up just felt right. "Emmett, you've got to see this. Here, let me kick down this blanket for you to climb. You can do it!"

Emmett had a strange realization: he didn't even care about seeing the top of Mount Couch at all, and he had no urge to climb. But he remembered that cats are all about "up," and he didn't want to be left down there all alone, so he gave it his best shot. Emmett stumbled clumsily over the blankets until he made it up to the top. And when he did, he was *scared*.

"I don't think I like mountains," Emmett said with a squeal, trying to find a safe way down as fast as possible. "I don't think 'up' is the place for me."

"Suit yourself, but you're one weird kitten," Jez said, jumping off Mount Couch with a swift and silent leap.

Jez's comment made Emmett squirm a bit, but he quickly brightened at a new thought: maybe this climbing obsession could work to his advantage. Even though Emmett may not have been interested in mountains, there was one thing he definitely liked, and that was searching for forbidden snacks. The other day, Emmett had found a mysterious, shiny door in the food room that seemed to hold treasures from the food lady, and he was dying to open it up and find the yumminess inside.

"What if we try going on a more . . . tasty adventure?" Emmett said. Jez agreed, and they jogged off to the kitchen, their mouths watering at the thought of snacks.

Once they'd made it to the kitchen, Emmett told Jez the plan. "I'll stand very still so you can climb on my back, just like you did at Mount Couch. Once you're up there, use your paws to tug on that shiny handle, and toss down what you find before the food fairy hears us. Just imagine the treasures!"

Jez nodded and hopped up on Emmett's back. The door was huge, but Jez was determined. He pulled and pulled until it finally gave way. Inside were huge piles of colorful foods, and Jez began to swat them all onto the floor as quickly as possible. "Teamwork makes the dream work!" he called down. "INCOMING!"

Perfectly ripe grapes rained from above. Broccoli florets scattered across the floor. A whole head of lettuce plopped out of a drawer. A case of strawberries tumbled off a shelf and sent juicy berries rolling all over. The kitchen was an absolute disaster!

Jez jumped down, sniffing at the supposed "treasures." There wasn't so much as a slice of lunch meat to be found! He watched his peculiar pink friend gobble up as many berries as he could possibly fit into his cheeks.

Emmett was in heaven, taking nibbles of every fruit and vegetable he could find. With a mouth full of leafy organic kale, he munched and shouted, "Jez, you've absolutely *got* to try this!"

"What?!" Jez said. "Have you *lost your mind*? We're *cats*, Emmett, not *bunny rabbits*!"

Stopping himself midchew, Emmett paused to think. *We're cats*, he told himself, and swallowed the greens with a

gulp. The last thing he wanted to do was seem like the odd kitten out.

"Oh, right. Totally. Like, where's the tuna?" Emmett huffed, trying not to notice the strawberry at his feet. He bopped it away with his hoof, inspiring a game of soccer.

They kicked bits of fruit all over the floor, and even though Emmett's snout was wiggling with desire, he resisted the urge to munch. After all, what business did a foster kitten have with berries, aside from practicing his hunt?

"Hey, Emmett, here's a joke. What do you call it when a couple of kittens raid the refrigerator and make a huge, huge mess?"

Jez paused a moment before he exclaimed, "A *catastrophe*. Get it? *Cat*-astrophe!"

Emmett let out a snort-laugh. "That's actually a really good one!"

CHAPTER 6

Bird-Watching

Exhausted from days filled with adventures, Emmett and Jez would fall into a cuddle-puddle night after night. Emmett was a deep sleeper, and all evening his tummy would rise and fall with every gentle snore. But Jez liked to take little catnaps through-out the day to make sure that he had the energy to hunt bugs through the window at dusk or to wake up at dawn with the rising sun.

After sleeping in one morning, Emmett lay on the bed alone, smacking his lips and yawning as daylight shined through the window. With half-open eyes, he peeked out from under heavy eyelashes. *Jez is surely off somewhere chasing a speck of light on the wall,* he thought, and sprawled out, somewhat pleased to have the bed to himself for a moment. Through the window, he gazed upon little lizards leaping over the rocks. He watched a butterfly gliding past. He noticed the trees blowing in the wind and remembered the feeling of the breeze against his face.

Three little songbirds fluttered onto

the ground, pecking at the earth. One picked up a worm in her beak, sang a happy tune, and flapped her wings with joy. Emmett lit up, pressing his nose against the glass to get a closer look. It looked like fun!

Soon the songbirds were singing and

chirping in perfect harmony. Emmett cleared his throat, warming up with a "me-me-me-me-me," and started to sing along. He sang his heart out, oinking low bass tones and squealing the high notes like a soprano. But his voice was muffled by the windowpane, and the birds could not hear him. Through a thick sheet of glass, he seemed to be a world away.

Oh, how he longed to feel the dirt beneath his hooves, to dig for worms, to be one with the birds and the breeze and the lizards and the . . .

"The bee?!" he called out as he noticed the bumblebee landing on a flower bush. Could it be? The same bee from the road?

"Bee! I'm in here!" Emmett called, but the bumblebee couldn't hear him. Emmett tapped on the glass with his hooves, eager to get her attention. *Tap, tap, tap!*

The bumblebee peeked out from behind a pink petal and gasped. "Emmett?" She flew toward him and placed her feet against the glass. "The little pig from the zzzide of the road? Izzz it really you?"

"It's me! Look! I made it to Fosterland!" he said loudly through the window. "It's amazing! Although"—he took a deep breath—"sometimes I do dream about the great outdoors. Maybe someday I can be out there in the field, singing in the sunshine with you and the birds . . . and my dear pal Jez!" He closed his eyes and smiled at the thought.

"That izzz a lovely dream. Who's Jezzz?" buzzed the bumblebee.

Emmett smiled. "Jez is my fluffy friend! He's the best. He's sweet, and funny, and—"

But before he could finish his sentence, he was interrupted by thundering growls and the sudden sound of Jez bounding down the hallway like the roof was on fire!

Slam! Jez smacked against the window with both paws. His eyes looked like saucers! "Let me at 'em! Let me at 'em!" Jez shouted. "I'll get that bumblebee. I swear I will! And those little birds, too!"

Startled by Jez's sudden pounce, the birds fluttered away, and the bumble-bee flew backward, vanishing into the wind.

"Jez!" Emmett stepped between him and the window, holding up a hoof. "The bee and the birds are our *friends*. And you scared them all away! Here, let's breathe together. In through the snout . . . out through the mouth . . . in through the snout . . ."

Jez took several deep breaths but kept the confused look on his face as he scratched his head. "The bees and birds are our *friends*?" Jez said. "You are one of a kind, Emmett. Sometimes

I wonder if you're even a kitten at all!"

Emmett gulped and forced a smile. Out of the corner of his eye, the pink reflection in the window was bothering him. He thought he could be a foster kitten—but the truth was, he was starting to doubt that, too.

Changing the subject, he turned the attention back to Jez, asking, "So, where have *you* been all morning?"

Jez's face lit up. "You won't believe me when I tell you. I got up this morning to use the litter box, and as I was trying to hide my poop—you know, so the food fairy doesn't steal it—I turned around and saw a jungle in the distance. A *jungle*, Emmett. There's a *giant tree*, two times the height of Mount Couch."

He continued. "I spent the whole morning trying to climb this thing. It isn't as easy, you know, with three legs, but I was determined. I gripped, and I clung, and I clawed, and finally—get this—I made it to the top. Emmett, it was the best. You can see everything from up there. Up high, in the treetops, life just feels right."

Emmett nodded as he listened to the tale. He found himself wondering how two close friends who loved each other so much could possibly manage to see the world from such different perspectives. Still, he was happy for Jez—really—even though his interests seemed so drastically different from his own.

CHAPTER 7

Faux Paws

In spite of their differences, Emmett and Jez were growing closer and closer. And not just because they went on so many adventures together but because Emmett was now *huge* and nearly squashed Jez every time they lay together on the cloud. He was now nearly three times the size of his friend.

"I can barely fit on this thing anymore,"

Jez whined one day, squished to the side. He laid his head on top of Emmett's giant pink tummy and sighed. "I'll never understand how you've grown so big when all you seem to eat is veggies and grains! Don't grow up too fast, my friend, or you'll be leaving Fosterland any day. . . ."

"Leaving Fosterland?" Emmett jolted up. "What are you even talking about?"

"Everyone knows Fosterland is just a temporary place. Right? I mean, didn't I ever tell you about . . . ?" Jez looked to his friend, who was flabbergasted. "Oh, shoot. I never finished reciting that rhyme, did I?"

Emmett slowly shook his head.

"Okay, here's the thing. . . . There's

another place we go after Fosterland."

Emmett's eyes grew huge. *"What?!"*

"Dang. I thought I told you. It's all in the rhyme."

Emmett furrowed his brows, completely confused.

Jez smacked his paw pad against his forehead. "Oops. See, the trouble is, I don't remember the whole rhyme. But I know someone who does. . . ."

They looked at each other and said in unison: "Coco the Elder Cat."

Off they went, over grasslands and through the jungle, searching for the wise black cat. They looked in the rain forest, but she wasn't there. They scoped out the grasslands, but they didn't see her anywhere. They checked Mount Couch, and Jez found little black hairs at the mountaintop—a sign she had been there not long ago.

"She's got to be around here some-where," Jez said, studying a piece of her fur.

Emmett looked to the windowsill, and

there she was, perched on a cushion in the sunlight, curled into a perfect circle.

"Psst!" Emmett whispered, pointing in her direction. "Found her!"

Jez's eyes lit up as they crept closer to Coco. "Ask her about the rhyme," he whispered.

"You ask," Emmett whispered back. Not only was he nervous to speak to Coco, but he was worried about what she'd say. Leave Fosterland? The only place he'd ever felt safe? Where he had met his best friend? Emmett didn't want to think about it.

"No, you ask!" Jez responded, nudging his friend.

"No, you!" Emmett said, nudging

Jez back and accidentally knocking him against the foot of a chair, which skidded across the floor. *Skrrrt.*

They both gasped and stood perfectly still.

The noise had awakened Coco from her snooze. She cracked open her watchful eyes, then lifted her long, lean neck from the cushion. She looked down at them, waiting for them to speak.

"Hello, ma'am. . . . If you don't mind . . . we just . . . had a quick . . . question," Jez started.

Coco sat perfectly still, listening.

Emmett cleared his throat. "We'd like to know what happens to foster kittens like us. Jez says there is a rhyme about Fosterland, and we'd like to hear it from start to finish. Please."

Coco looked at Emmett and winked. She stood and stretched up tall, so shiny and sleek, and slowly recited the rhyme:

"Dream big, dream big,
and soon you'll see
All that a foster grows to be.
The dream inside your heart today
Decides the place you go to stay.
Fosterland is but a phase
To foreshadow the best of days.
For all your dreams will
soon come true,
When Foreverland welcomes you."

And with that, she curled back into a
ball and fell asleep.

"Foreverland?" Emmett said. "What in
the . . . ?"

Jez leaned in. "What I was trying to tell

you is . . . this isn't a permanent home. There is another place for us—a forever home made just for us out of our hopes and wishes."

Emmett squinted, trying to make sense of it all.

Jez continued. "Don't you see? That's the magic of being a foster kitten. When you're a foster kitten in Fosterland, you can lie on this fluffy cloud to let your imagination soar and think about the life you hope to live. Our dreams travel up into the sunbeam and swirl around over our heads, making our future bright! Dream big, because your dreams are designing your future life in Foreverland!"

"The dream inside your heart today . . . ," Emmett pondered. "So you're saying that the things we dream about today will decide where we end up going for good?"

Jez nodded. "Yes, something like that."

"And we'll go to the same Foreverland?"

"I don't see why not," Jez said. "We're best friends!"

"Well, then I dream that Foreverland has fluffy pillows!"

"Yes!" said Jez. "I'm right there with you. Oh, and sunny spots!"

"I *love* sunny spots!" Emmett replied.

"I dream Foreverland has a wrestling ring and lots of good snacks," Jez continued.

"Definitely. Snacks are a *must*. Like crunchy lettuce, and—ooh! Water-melon." Emmett's mouth was watering just imagining it.

"I was thinking tuna, but okay," Jez said, laughing.

"I dream Foreverland has lots of birds who want to sing songs with me."

"There you go with birds again. I don't need birds in Foreverland, but I wouldn't mind a couple of feathers dangling from a string. . . ."

"You have weird hobbies, Jez," Emmett said, huffing. The last thing he wanted to do was insult his friend, but seriously, *what was with this guy?*

"Em," Jez said, "all I want is a tall tree

where I can survey my kingdom. My dream is that Foreverland has an epic treetop view."

"Who wants to be way up there? I can't even *see* up there," Emmett said. "I dream that Foreverland is filled with dirt and worms!"

"Dirt is gross," Jez said, licking his paw.

"You're gross! You lick your own butt!" Emmett said, grumbling.

"Yeah, Emmett, because I'm a kitten. What kind of kitten *doesn't* lick their own butt?"

Emmett felt his heart sink. All at once, a terrible feeling came over him, a feeling he had buried and tried to forget. But now it was bubbling to the surface faster than he could stop the words from escaping his mouth—

"Well, maybe I'm *not* a foster kitten! Maybe I'm a . . . I'm a . . . a . . . pig!"

"What are you talking about?" Jez laughed.

"I'm a pig, Jez. I think I'm a pig." Emmett thought back to the bumblebee's words and the fact that his reflection looked so different from his kitten best friend's. He felt in his heart that the bee was right. He was a pig.

Jez blinked, speechless. In his shock, every hair on his body stuck straight out as if he'd been hit by lightning. He looked like a prickly pine cone as he arched his back, stunned, and sidestepped out of the room.

Emmett looked down, watching a teardrop fall to the floor. He'd finally admitted what he might have known all along. That he was *not* a foster kitten at all but was actually a *piglet*.

The truth was, the only thing he knew about being a pig was that it was scary and lonely. He could hear the words of the bumblebee echoing in his brain: "Little pig, bee careful!" Deep down he'd always worried about going back to those feelings of hunger, of thirst, of loneliness and fear.

His life had only started to get better once he found out he was, in fact, a foster kitten. Being a kitten was the only thing that ever felt safe! Now that he'd confessed the truth, his head was swimming with the sinking feeling that maybe he was about to lose everything. Including his best friend.

Just as he was feeling like he couldn't be more alone, Jez slowly turned the corner and walked in with his tail between his legs.

"What do you call it when a kitten rudely storms out on his best friend?" He hung his head in shame. "A faux paw." He smiled shyly and swished his tail onto Emmett's face, wiping away his tears. "I'm sorry, Emmett. I didn't know what to say. I'm sorry."

Emmett took a deep breath. "I forgive you," he sniffled. "Besides . . . I guess I'm the one with the fake paws. . . ." He tried to joke, holding up one leg, but his hoof was trembling. "So what does this mean?"

"I think"—Jez gulped, staring into the distance—"if I'm a kitten . . . and you're a pig . . . and we have very different dreams . . . I think it means that we might be going to different Foreverlands."

CHAPTER 8

Meoink

The truth was out.

All along, Emmett had been a baby pig, not a kitten. And that explained all his quirks—his fear of heights, his love of vegetables, and his gentle fondness for birds and other creatures. All the things he thought made him strange weren't actually weird at all for a piglet. But the problem was that he and his friend Jez had different dreams, which seemed sure to lead them down different paths.

"I've been thinking," Jez said, hopping up onto Emmett's back. "If the dreams we dream today decide the place we go to stay, then all we have to do . . . is dream the same dreams!"

Emmett wasn't so sure.

"Hear me out," Jez said. "If we want to stay together, all we have to do is prove to the food fairy that we are exactly alike. She's in charge of this place, after all. If we can show her that we have the same exact dreams, then she's bound to send us to the same Foreverland! And if you can't be a kitten, then maybe I, Jez, can learn how to be a pig. Why not? I bet I can do it!"

Emmett felt a flutter of hope. ". . . So you want to be a pig now?"

"How hard can it be? Here, teach me how to say something in 'pig.'"

Emmett let out a long, slow "ooooiiiink," then looked at Jez, who was studying his mouth intently. "Okay, now you try."

Jez took a deep breath and gave it his best shot. "Meeeeoooink!"

Emmett smiled.

"Meoink! Meoink! Meoink! Am I doing it? That's the best I can do. Meoink!"

Emmett gave a knowing nod. "Maybe we can try something else. Want to sample some kale?" He nosed open the food box, which he was now tall enough to reach on his own, and pulled out a leafy green. "I know it looks funky, but trust me when I say it's delicious," Emmett told his friend.

Jez plugged his nose, opened wide, and stuffed the whole leaf into his frowning mouth. With his mouth full, he gagged and said, "Yop . . . dis tashtes like . . . um . . . grash-flavored construshin papor. . . ."

Just then the food fairy walked into the room. Jez immediately snapped into character and let out a big "MEOINK!" while green drool spilled out from his cheeks. "Yum, dat kale ish vewy tashty shtuff!" he called out, shoving another leaf into his mouth. "Meoink! Meoink!"

The food fairy kneeled down and pet

them each on the head lovingly, then walked away.

Spitoo! Jez spat out the big green ball of mush and looked over to his friend. "Do you think we convinced her?"

CHAPTER 9

The Mirror

The next morning, Jez awoke sprawled across Emmett's head. With a big stretch and a yawn, he mumbled, "I tried to dream of birds and breeze, but all I could see was tuna and trees. It's hard to tell yourself what to dream."

Emmett sat up slowly, and Jez rolled onto the bed, looking up at his big pig friend. They were each so tiny when they first met, but in their time together both of them had grown a lot. Sitting tall, Emmett was struck by the feeling that growth doesn't just happen on the outside—it's also something that happens on the *inside*, where you slowly find out who you really are and stop trying to be who you really aren't. Emmett looked at his kitten friend and said:

"Don't dream for me, Jez—dream for yourself. Dreams should be easy, I think . . ." Emmett paused, thinking back to his attempts at kittenhood. "Trust me, I know what it's like to try to dream someone else's dream. Remember when I tried to climb Mount Couch with *these*?" He held up his hooves, and they both giggled. "I mean . . . *talk about awkward*!" Emmett chuckled. "I was just trying to fit in. But now I realize it's kind of awesome that we are a little different. It makes us unique!"

"Come with me," Emmett said. He walked toward the rain forest, and Jez followed behind. Heading straight to the steamy mirror, Emmett said, "Ready?"

On the count of three, they wiped away the dew with their paws and snoot, revealing a crystal-clear image of a small brown kitten and a large pink piglet standing side by side. "It's us!" they both said in awe.

Jez said, "Emmett, I owe you an

apology. I spent so much time telling you to be more like me! I was wrong. You've got such an incredible snout, and your tail is so cool. Emmett, you're a marvel. And you're my friend. You're a perfect piglet. You deserve all the mud and berries you can dream of."

Emmett looked at himself, and for the first time ever, he didn't want to look away. He noticed his height and thought it was impressive indeed. He noticed his snout, so round and handsome. He turned to the side and observed his little skinny tail, which he actually thought looked quite cute when it wiggled about.

He said to his friend, "Jez, you're one cool cat. You've taught me so much about how to have a friend. So what if you're into different stuff than I am? Look at your whiskers and your striking paws. You run faster on three legs than I can on four! You're going to make a fantastic king of a jungle someday."

Jez inhaled deeply. He could see that his back limb was strong and muscular and that his mane was growing in thick and silky. And he could see that he had indeed grown into a majestic young cat.

Emmett kneeled down, setting his face right next to Jez's, and they took in their reflections. Four eyes, seven legs, two mouths, one nose, one snout, and two giant, hope-filled hearts.

Emmett whispered softly, "Even if

we're a little different, we're the same in all the ways that matter, and we always will be."

Emmett and Jez wandered over to the grasslands and lay sprawled on the floor, looking up at the ceiling. Emmett cuddled in close, feeling overcome by the happy-sad, nervous-excited feeling that a new chapter was soon to begin.

Breaking the silence, he asked, "What do you think Foreverland is like?"

Jez thought for a moment. "Well," he responded, "Foreverland is what you dream it's going to be. So I think it's going to be a dream come true—for me and for you."

A dream come true, Emmett thought,

and began to let his mind wander. . . .

After a moment, he let out a contented little grunt. "Rrrruh."

"What's that sound, Em?" Jez asked.

"I think it's the sound pigs make when they're happy," Emmett replied. "It's like a purr, in pig language. Rrrruh."

And there they lay, purring and grunting in peace.

CHAPTER 10

The Train Car

A few days later, they noticed the arrival of something new. It was a rectangular plastic container with little windows on the side and a handle on top. They sniff-sniff-sniffed around it. *What is it?* Emmett wondered.

Jez walked inside. "Aha! Interesting . . . ," he said.

Emmett tried to walk in, but only his head would fit.

"I've seen one of these before," Jez exclaimed. "It's some kind of train car! The last time I saw one, it was here to take other foster kittens off to Foreverland. Could it be . . . that it's here for one of us?"

Emmett bonked his head against the top of the carrier. "Well, I don't fit. I don't think it's here for me. I guess that means . . ."

Jez sat up tall, his eyes wide. "It's . . . for me?"

Emmett nodded. He felt sad, but he knew that the right thing to do was to celebrate his friend's big moment. Tapping his toes, he said, "Jez, this is such a special day! Okay, what can I do to help you prepare?"

Jez paced, speaking faster and faster. "Oh my word. This is so exciting. Okay, let's see. First, we need to pack all my things. I'll need three little rattle mice, two jingle balls, and a feather toy. I absolutely must pack a few cans of my favorite snacks. And what about the tree? Can I take that with me? Who am I kidding. It's *Foreverland*! They probably have *ten trees*! Oh, I hope they like me there. How do I look? Are my whiskers neat? Is my coat shiny?" He licked his paws and slicked back the fur on his cheeks.

"You are beyond ready! I'm so happy for you." Emmett paused and smiled. "And I dare say, my friend, you look . . . *purrfect*."

"Oh my gosh. Did you just come up with a cat joke?!" Jez laughed hysterically.

"What can I say? I guess you taught me a thing or two about kittens." Emmett smiled.

Jez jumped around Emmett's neck, giving him a long, fluffy hug.

Knock, knock, knock.

The food fairy opened the door, and four feet stepped into the house.

Jez looked upward and couldn't believe his eyes. Two humans were kneeling in his direction. And they had gifts! When he approached them to say hello, they pet him under his chin in *exactly* the right spot. They pulled out a wand toy, and he went absolutely bananas! He frolicked and jumped and showed off his incredible pounce. Then the two new giants pulled out a tuna snack. He was in disbelief. How did they know about all his favorite things?

Emmett watched, grinning from ear to ear. It was a warm smile—the one you make when you see your best friend achieving their dream. Jez had dreamed up the perfect family, and now they were here to take him home to Foreverland. How could he be anything but happy for his friend?

Jez stepped into the train car but then

looked out at Emmett, raising a paw against the bars. "I'll miss you, Emmett!"

As the giants carried Jez out, Emmett ran to the door to get a final glimpse of his friend. The first and only best friend he had ever had.

And Emmett was left alone to sit on the cloud and dream of his own future.

CHAPTER 11

A Dream Come True

Dreaming was fun when Emmett thought he was a kitten, but it felt a lot scarier as a pig. Emmett knew exactly what his heart wanted, but he had never heard of a piglet's dreams coming true, so it felt a little scary to dream at all. Was there a Foreverland for pigs? Was there a train car big enough to take him there?

He thought about falling from the truck and the realization that a mere bump in the road can change your life forever. He remembered the fear he felt when he was scooped up by a giant and the terror of seeing Jez's claws for the first time. Change can be scary. But change also brought him to Fosterland.

This was the spot he'd spent so many days sending his wishes into the sunbeam and so many nights asleep by Jez's side. As Emmett drifted off to sleep, he couldn't help but wonder if a perfect life for a pig really *was* just a dream. He looked out the window at the trees swaying in the breeze and drifted off to sleep.

Whoosh.

Emmett felt a strange sensation, as if he were floating. The cloud bed seemed to lift and lift, soaring into the air.

Am I dreaming?

The cloud bed was taking him down the hallway and toward the front door, which he had entered when he was just a baby.

Am I asleep or awake? Is this it? Am I leaving Fosterland?

The door creaked open, and as Emmett zoomed through the exit, he noticed a new train car was arriving, carrying a small gray kitten. Passing her on the side-walk, he locked eyes with the kitten and longed to tell her that she was safe—to head for the sunbeam and make a wish!

"Dream big!" he called out as he glided past her, but before she could answer, the door had closed behind him—and he had officially left Fosterland.

He found himself in the lap of the food fairy, with trees zipping past him at lightning speed yet again, just like when he had first arrived.

He closed his eyes, whispering to himself. *Dream big, Emmett. Dream big. All your dreams will soon come true.* . . . He hoped the words were true, but his only experience outside Fosterland was a lonely ditch on the side of the road, and he didn't want to go back there.

His heart was pounding with every thump in the road. For a long while, he sat in the passenger seat, wincing and wishing. What can a pig do but hope for the best?

Finally, the vehicle came to a stop. As the car door opened, he heard the most beautiful sound. . . .

A whole chorus of happy animals was singing a song—just for him!

"Welcome, Emmett!
Chirp and moo!
Baah and gobble—
cluck cluck, too!
A welcome song that's
just for you.
Foreverland is a dream
come true!"

He looked out at the pasture. Could it be? His heart was fluttering like a butterfly in flight. His dream! His dream had come true! He had made it to Foreverland, and it was everything he'd wanted and more. Bees buzzed, birds flapped about, and goats greeted him with friendly nudges. Jez had been right all along. The dreams he'd dreamed had led him to his perfect home.

He ran into the grassy pasture, which felt wonderful under his hooves. Spinning and jumping for joy, Emmett zoomed to and fro, feeling the dirt under his hooves, letting the breeze flow against his pink peach fuzz, and eagerly greeting the other animals.

Taking it all in, he called out to the sun with a loud, happy "OINK." A moment later, he heard the sound echoing back to him. "Oink—oink!"

He called out again: "OINK! OINK OINK OINK!"

And a moment later, he heard the echo again. "Oink! Oink oink oink. Oink! Oink oink oink."

Well, that's funny! he thought. *How does a voice echo in an open field?*

He trotted in the direction of the sound and called out once more. "OINK?"

Dozens of oinks were calling back to him, and his little hooves picked up speed as he got closer and closer to the fence.

Then Emmett gasped. Through the

fencing he could see that there were dozens of beings who looked just like him. Pink pigs, black pigs, and even pigs with spots and dots. Pigs with tusks that framed their smiles. And giant pigs twenty times his size!

A black pig who Emmett would later learn was Joshua, the leader of the bunch, gave Emmett a nod from across the yard, then went back to chomping away at a pumpkin.

"It's a dream come true," Emmett whispered to himself.

Emmett trotted along the fence, nose-to-knee with all the big pigs. He could see that a happy world for pigs is possible indeed.

CHAPTER 12

A Forever Friend

"Bzz, bzz!" said the bee floating above Emmett's head. Months had passed in Foreverland, and Emmett was a teen pig now, with lanky legs and a cool spiky Mohawk, which stood straight up as the bee zipped around him.

"Bzz, bzz! The buzz around town is that Jez is the king of his own houzzze!" the bee told Emmett. "I tried to zzzay hello to him through the window, but he pounzzzed against the glazzz!"

Emmett giggled. "Did he look happy?"

The bee landed on Emmett's nose and told him, "Azzz happy as a pig in mud! And guezzz what! He'zzz got a cat for a friend!"

Emmett smiled. *Jez deserves a wonderful friend,* he thought.

In his own Foreverland, Emmett was far from lonely. He would sing with the birds, dance with the sheep, and call out to the barn cat from across the field: "Hey, David! Meoink!" Even though he hadn't quite made a close bond with another pig just yet—they were all so very *big* compared to him, after all—he was friendly with everyone, and new animals were showing up all the time, too.

Emmett loved to stand by the gate to greet newcomers and had become the official head of the Foreverland Welcoming Committee. Over the months he had welcomed a handful of new kids who looked up to him for his storytelling and kindness and had assembled a little gang of goat friends who followed him everywhere.

And so there he found himself, playing and foraging with the goat kids near the front gate, when he noticed that the food fairy was at the door. *What is she doing here?* he wondered. In her arms, she held a cloud bed just like the one he'd slept on all his life, except his was now caked with dirt from the farm, and the one in her arms was fresh and clean, like it had just come straight out of Fosterland. . . .

The food fairy kneeled to the ground, and a gray piglet hopped off the cloud and ran right up to Emmett, squealing. Emmett couldn't believe it. She had brought another young pig, just like him!

Oh, he was so excited! As he reached out a hoof to introduce himself, the piglet interrupted:

"Emmett! It's you! It's really you! I've heard so much about you."

"You . . . know my name?" asked Emmett, confused.

"Of course I know your name! You're, like, a legend in Fosterland!"

Emmett's eyes lit up. "I am?"

"Oh yeah, the cats talk about you all the time. Emmett Pig, friend of kittens! Friend of all animals! You paved the way for pigs like me to dream of a future like this. I'm Hugo. I was raised with foster kittens, too. And I've always dreamed that someday I could be your friend. I've been counting the days till I could meet you!"

"You have?" Emmett's tail was really wagging now. He looked at Hugo, who was beaming, and said, "Hugo, welcome. I have a feeling we're going to be the best of pals."

From that moment on, Emmett and
Hugo were inseparable. During the day,
they'd romp through the mud, eat fresh
veggies in the sunshine, and swap stories of their former feline foster friends.

"Fowever fwiendsh!" Hugo said one
day with a mouthful of pumpkin pulp,
and Emmett laughed.

"That's right. Friends forever," Emmett
grunted happily.

At night, they'd sleep on their cloud beds side by side. Goat friends would rest their sleepy heads on the edge of the clouds, and Emmett would share bedtime stories of his adventures in Fosterland.

"Tell us again about how you climbed Mount Couch! How on earth did you get up?" a goat asked once.

"Up? What's 'up'?" a pig muttered from across the field, and Emmett and Hugo looked at each other and smiled.

A Few Weeks Later ...

Emmett was lying in the sunshine when Hugo came galloping in his direction.

"THIS IS NOT A DRILL!" Hugo shouted, running. "Alert! Alert! This is a code red alert!"

Emmett opened his eyes. "What? What's going on?"

"We are needed at the gate *immediately*! There is a new train car here, and,

Emmett . . . it's filled with KITTENS! No one knows how to talk to them," he said. "This is a job only we can do! Hurry!"

Emmett leapt up, and together they reached the gate, where eight little kittens were huddled together, trembling.

"Welcome, little ones!" Emmett spoke softly. "Have no fear. I know *a lot* about being a kitten. Come with us. We'll show you all the ropes." Underneath a big oak tree, he told them true tales of kitten adventures of jungles and cat trees and of dreams come true—all the while thinking of his cat friend, Jez.

His tail was wagging from side to side, and the kittens thought it was the silliest thing they'd ever seen. *Pounce!* They jumped and played with his tail, no longer afraid.

The little kittens began to purr. *I love that sound,* Emmett thought, and let out a happy grunt. "Rrrruh!"

Hugo grunted back. "Rrrruh! Rrrruh!"

Soon the whole group was sprawled over Emmett, purring and grunting in happiness.

"Do you like cat jokes?" he asked, and the kittens nodded with eyes wide.

"Here's a classic from my friend Jez. What do you call a pile of kittens?"

The kittens looked at him lovingly, eager to hear the punchline.

". . . A meowntain!"

Underneath the tree, the kittens and piglets laughed and laughed.

The True Story of Emmett and Jez

Emmett was found on the side of the road in El Cajon, California, when he was just hours old. Shortly after being rescued, he was brought to my non-profit, Orphan Kitten Club, which rescues orphaned baby animals in need Never had I ever seen a piglet so sma' When he arrived in my care, he weigh less than a pound and was so hun and happy to slurp down a dish of v

goat milk. After he settled in, he met my then-foster kitten Jez, who was about five weeks old and slightly bigger than him at the time. Jez was recovering from a hind limb amputation and didn't have any other kitten friends. Almost instantly they connected and became pals.

In foster care, Emmett and Jez had a hilarious and adorable friendship. Emmett learned to play with cat toys and run through the house with his friend, causing all sorts of mayhem. They chatted to each other constantly, even though they spoke totally different languages. Once they were sleepy, they'd always curl up together on their pink bed. As they grew up, Emmett quickly eclipsed Jez in size;

while cats grow to be about ten pounds, potbelly pigs eventually grow to one hundred fifty pounds or more!

Once Emmett and Jez were big and strong, it was time for them to find loving forever homes. So many people asked if I would adopt Emmett and Jez out together, but the truth is that even though they loved each other, they had very different needs. Jez was a three-legged indoor kitten who craved interaction with another cat, and Emmett was a soon-to-be-giant pig who longed for outdoor enrichment and other pig friends.

Jez found a loving adopter in Los Angeles, where he is now renamed

Puck and lives with a friendly tuxedo cat named Wolfgang. Emmett found placement at a wonderful vegan farm animal sanctuary in Campo, California, called Farm Animal Refuge, where he still lives to this day. And about six months after Emmett went to his forever home, I fostered another little orphaned piglet, Hugo, who eventually became Emmett's best friend—forever! I still visit them frequently and smile knowing that Emmett is truly getting to live his dream life.